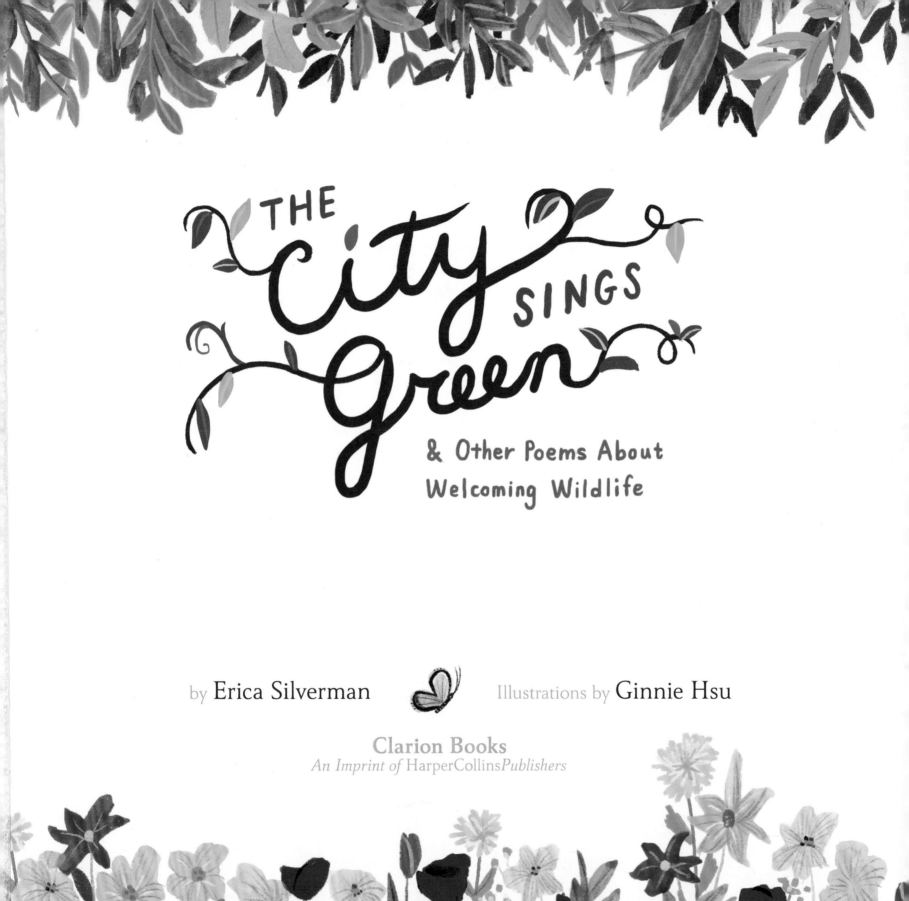

THE City SINGS Green

& Other Poems About Welcoming Wildlife

by Erica Silverman   Illustrations by Ginnie Hsu

Clarion Books
An Imprint of HarperCollinsPublishers

For all of you, young and old, who are
rewilding your city—plant by plant, bird by bird,
creature by creature, river by river—
you are an inspiration.
—E.S.

For Kyle, Luna, and Boba.
—G.H.

Clarion Books is an imprint of HarperCollins Publishers.

The City Sings Green & Other Poems About Welcoming Wildlife
Text copyright © 2024 by Erica Silverman
Illustrations copyright © 2024 by Ginnie Hsu
All rights reserved. Manufactured in Italy.
No part of this book may be used or reproduced in any manner whatsoever without written permission
except in the case of brief quotations embodied in critical articles and reviews. For information address
HarperCollins Children's Books, a division of HarperCollins Publishers, 195 Broadway, New York, NY 10007.
www.harpercollinschildrens.com

Library of Congress Control Number: 2023937614
ISBN 978-0-35-843456-6

The artist used acrylic gouache on paper and scanned to edit digitally to create the illustrations for this book.
Design by Phil Caminiti and Honee Jang
24 25 26 27 28 RTLO 10 9 8 7 6 5 4 3 2 1
First Edition

TABLE OF CONTENTS

THE CITY SINGS GREEN

Green me, sings the City.
Dig my dirt and seed me.
Plant my streets, my yards, my lots
with native shrubs and trees.

Clean me, sings the City.
Take out the trash.
Remove the fumes.
Purge all poisons from my soil.

Rewild me, sings the City.
Then watch
        what grows, what flows,
            what flutters, flies, soars,
                slithers, dives, crawls.
Watch what perches
            in unexpected places.

Watch what comes,
enters your heart,
and stays.

Rewild me, sings the City,
and I will
rewild
you.

More than four billion people live in cities around the world, and that number is growing. Cities are spreading out, bulldozing wilderness, and destroying forests, deserts, and other wild lands where animals live. As a result, a million species, from life-supporting plants to tiny insects to large mammals, face extinction.

But city people around the world are finding creative solutions to stop extinction and make cities more livable for wildlife.

YOUR RIVER   The Bronx, New York City, USA

Bronx –
This was your river:

refrigerators, shopping carts,
  carburetors, piano parts,
    tea kettles, bottles, pans,
  bike pedals, rusty cans,
    worn-out shoes, plates, spoons,

TVs, crates, chairs, balloons,
  motherboards, tangled wires,
thousands and thousands and
  thousands of tires.

You waded in, mucked about.
  Hands gloved, you carried it all out!

You, Bronx,
    you
  restored the water
and the shore, planted
white oak, sycamore,
soft rush, elderberry,
spicebush, wild cherry.

Now
    in the shadow of the passing trains,
honking horns, clanking cranes,
    your river beckons.
    Fish flitter.
        Frogs hide in the shade.
            Turtles glide. Herons wade.

By the banks of your river,
anything is possible.
Even this nose-wriggling,
dam-building, long-missing
beaver
finding his way
home.

For centuries, the Bronx River flowed through Lenape land, providing a habitat for thriving beaver families. But the European colonists overhunted them for their pelts until few remained. As streets replaced forest, the last beavers vanished from the Bronx. The river became a polluted dumping ground.

Bronx residents organized a massive cleanup of their river, starting in the 1980s. It was so successful that, in 2007, a beaver returned to the Bronx River for the first time in almost three hundred years!

FOR THE BEES Oslo, Norway

"Keep 'em buzzing!"
        That was our goal.
We built them
        a honeybee highway,
        a pollinator parkway,
        a flowering flyway,

                Set up
                rest stops,
                        sipping spots,
                        food pots
                serving pollen and nectar

Turned buildings that were roadblocks
        into
        sweet plots
        on
walkways, rooftops, patios, parking lots,

Put
a bee box here,
a meadow there,
bowls of marigold, snapdragon, violet, daisy
everywhere

Now stopping
atop a tall building,
honey makers
check in

to a bee hotel
    with a bee buffet
        where open-faced sunflowers
        sway
            as if to say—
    Welcome, Bees! Welcome to Oslo!

More than thirty percent of our food depends on honeybees. As they zip around gathering nectar, bees spread pollen to fruits and vegetables. But pesticides, climate change, and habitat destruction are killing them off. In cities, habitat fragmentation makes it hard for bees to reach the food, water, and shelter they need to survive.

In Norway, where one-third of bee species are endangered, people created a special bee "highway" that stretches from one end of Oslo to the other. Bee boxes, flower gardens, roof gardens, flowerpots, and water fountains provide places for bees to rest and refuel every eight hundred feet.

IN OUR SCHOOLYARD

Los Angeles, California, USA

Here in our schoolyard, surrounded
by skyscrapers, apartment buildings,
the *thrmmm* of traffic,
the *vvvrrrrrmmm* of choppers,

we removed the blacktop

planted oak, poppy, sage,
all that once grew wild,
before the city built itself up and
spread itself out.

In this oasis that we made,
we watched them arrive—
hummingbirds, bees, butterflies,
lizards, warblers, doves . . .

We watched, sketched,
asked how, what, why,
and just when we thought
    it doesn't get any better than this . . .

there
on the branch of a coral tree,
the startled eyes
of a tiny
spotted-brown
burrowing owl
blinked at us

and

we

blinked

back.

The Esperanza School in downtown Los Angeles decided to rewild their schoolyard. Guided by their principal, Brad Rumble, and working with local environmental groups, they removed about four thousand feet of asphalt and planted California native shrubs and trees. One November day, fourth-grade birder Nathan Hobb spotted a burrowing owl—a rare sighting—in their schoolyard habitat!

Once abundant in southern California, this owl became scarce as roads and buildings replaced desert and grassland. For the school's many students of Guatemalan descent, the owl is a symbol of luck, and this lucky owl found a perch in downtown Los Angeles thanks to their hard work. The students were so excited, they decided to change the school mascot from a dragon to a burrowing owl!

THE LITTLE BLACK REDSTARTS OF LONDON TOWN

London, United Kingdom

oh, the little Black Redstarts of London town
    are losing ground
    as the city grows up
    their numbers go down
whatever shall we do?

oh the little Black Redstarts of London town
    lived in rubble-filled lots
    until buildings rose up
    on all of their plots
whatever shall we do?

now the little Black Redstarts
    have no place to feed
    no place to forage
    for worm, bug, and seed
whatever shall we do?

Let's build them a green roof
a home way up high
with flowers and insects
surrounded by sky
oh that's what we shall do

oh the little Black Redstarts
now can be found
pecking and nesting
high above ground
on the lovely green roofs of London town.

For many years, the black redstart made its home in the ruins of buildings bombed during World War II. When the city began building on these lots, the black redstarts lost their habitat and their numbers declined. Worried that these songbirds would go extinct, a London birder created green roofs on top of buildings. Made of crushed concrete, compressed sand, and brick covered with sedum and native wildflowers, green roofs provide food and shelter for black redstarts. As one of Britain's rarest birds, it is a protected species.

THERE ONCE WERE RAVENS

Toronto, Canada

There once were trees for ravens to nest in.
We cut down the trees.

There once were creatures for ravens to feast on.
We poisoned the creatures.

There once were crops for ravens to feed on.
We shot the ravens.

When did the last one leave?
Did we mourn?
Did we cheer?

The ravens remembered, warned their young:
Stay away!
Stay away!

But in the years' long silence of lost song
something inside us
shifted.

Missing trees, we grew a forest.
Missing creatures, we shunned poison.
Missing ravens, we lay down our guns.

The ravens knew.

Look!
On the chimney of a power generator
in downtown Toronto
    ravens
        are nesting!

Farmland outside the city of Toronto was once dangerous territory for ravens. When farmers poisoned wolves and other predators to protect their livestock, ravens ate the poisoned carcasses and died. When ravens ate their crops, farmers shot them.

The ravens moved north to wilder lands.

But recently, Toronto has been creating green spaces and urban forests. City people do not shoot ravens.

In fact, many have become fans of these intelligent birds.

In 2014, for the first time in over one hundred years, a raven's nest was spotted in an industrial area of Toronto. It marked the beginning of the ravens' return.

POSSUMS CONSIDER A ROPE BRIDGE

Busselton, Australia

We should not travel the road below.
It's a dangerous place for us possums to go.
But our *here* was split off from our *there*.

We used to scurry, leap and roam.
From branch to branch in our forest home.
Now we gaze down at the road below.

Someone felled our peppermint trees
and left a wide gap in our canopy.
Our here was split off from our there.

But wait! What's this? How mysterious!
A bridge? For us? We're curious.
It stretches above the road below.

But dare we trust it? Is it strong?
It's high. It's wide. It's very long.
Will it get us from here to there?

Yes! Now we can roam our canopy home.
We can leap and scurry everywhere.
No need to travel the road below
   with our rope bridge from here to there!

High in Australia's forest canopy, the western ringtail possum travels by leaping from tree to tree.
When trees are removed to build highways, the possums can't move around their territory.
Many are injured or killed trying to cross streets and roads.

In Busselton, Sydney, and other Australian cities, scientists have partnered with city governments
to build rope bridges high above busy streets and highways, connecting divided habitats. The
bridges, made of two poles connected with a wire-and-mesh swing, provide safe passage not only
for possums, but also for squirrel gliders, sugar gliders, and tree kangaroos.

TO THE MIGRATING BIRDS OF THE MISSISSIPPI FLYWAY

Chicago, Illinois, USA

Yellow Warblers, Virginia Rails,
Dark-Eyed Juncos, Northern Pintails,
Golden Eagles, Swallow-Tailed Kites—
Be wary of Chicago nights!

We're sorry that our city lights
 outshine the stars
 and pull you off flight.

We're sorry that our high-rise buildings
 and clear glass windows
 confuse your sight.

We didn't know you might collide,
 fall, get hurt,
die.

Seaside Sparrows, Blue-Winged Teals,
Barn Owls, Barred Owls, Whip-Poor-Wills.
Black-Legged Kittiwakes, Sandhill Cranes—
 We're doing what we can to change.

We're turning off lights,
 so you can read the stars
  by the dark of night.

We're marking up windows, pulling down shades
 to warn you: Stop, Birds!
  Glass ahead! Veer away!

But should you collide, should you get hurt,
 we will seek you, heal you, release you—
  We are on constant alert.

Tufted Titmice, Sanderlings,
Grackles, Willets, Bobolinks,
Red-Winged Blackbirds, Common Loons—
Migrate safely by the stars and moon.

Every spring and fall, millions of birds migrate the Mississippi Flyway from South America to Canada. When they fly over cities, they face danger from city lights and window glass.
   Thanks to Lights Out Chicago, ninety to one hundred percent of buildings voluntarily turn off their lights between eleven p.m. and sunrise during migration. People pull down blinds or use bird tape, decals, or soap to mark windows so birds can see the glass and turn away. When birds crash into buildings, the Chicago Bird Collision Monitors are ready. These dedicated volunteers search downtown streets to find injured birds and bring them to a rehabilitation center.

SMALL AND SHIMMERY

El Segundo, California, USA

We are the small and shimmery
   El Segundo Blues.
Once in swarms, we flutter-flew
   along the coast, among the dunes
where seacliff buckwheat bloomed.
   Until—

The BULLDOZERS rumbled in,
    trampling flowers, toppling bluffs.
Then an airport, houses, streets popped up.

The city built out everywhere,
and our seacliff buckwheat disappeared.

Going.
    Going.
        We were
            almost
                gone . . .

But on one lonely piece of sand
    near lanes where groaning airplanes land,
rare clumps of seacliff buckwheat grew.
    So we hung on.
Until—

Some people found us,
    understood our need for food
and home. With caring hands,
    they spread sweet buckwheat
and restored the dunes.

27

These days we feed on nectar,
          lay our eggs.
Our caterpillars munch on flower heads,
          then curl into chrysalides,
and sleep beneath the buckwheat plant
          and wake
               as
               butterflies.
                    We,
               the El Segundo Blues,
                    are on the rise!

The El Segundo Blue Butterfly was the first insect to go on the Endangered Species List. This species cannot survive without seacliff buckwheat (also called dune or coast buckwheat). Adults feed on the nectar, then lay their eggs on the flower heads. The caterpillar eats the seeds. The chrysalides, or pupae, sleep in the soil under the plant. As the Pacific coast dunes were paved over, the buckwheat died off, and the butterfly faced extinction. But when a few butterflies were discovered in a small surviving patch of seacliff buckwheat near Los Angeles International Airport, conservationists were thrilled. Habitat restoration began. Now there are more than nine recovery areas. Although still endangered, there is hope for the El Segundo Blue Butterfly.

LITTLE BLUE PENGUINS

Oamaru, New Zealand

Dear Little Blues of Oamaru—
Look what we
have built for you—
a lighted tunnel
beneath the highway
No more worries!
No need to hurry!
Waddle safely!
Dawdle, do!
Dear Little Blues of Oamaru

Dear Little Blues of Oamaru—
We fretted as you
crossed the highway,
trembled as you
dashed through traffic
Cars so fast!
Trucks so big!
Do not dawdle!
Quickly waddle!

At about fourteen inches high, Little Blue or Kokora penguins are the world's smallest penguins. They are endangered by oil spills, plastic pollution, habitat loss, and traffic.

In the seaside city of Oamaru, in New Zealand, Little Blues had to cross a dangerous highway daily to get from their nesting site to the ocean to feed on small fish. A marine biologist designed an eighty-foot tunnel under the highway to protect them from traffic. The people of Oamaru helped get it built. The penguins quickly learned to use the tunnel. In most of New Zealand and Australia, their numbers

OTTER CITY   Singapore

Your gleaming buildings
        were on the rise.
Our wetland home was
        in demise.
Garbage clogged our
        waterways.
We, your otters,
        couldn't stay.

        But you restored the rivers,
                dredged them clean.
        Planted trees.
                Turned the city green.

We came back! We've arrived!
        We are your prize!
                What an utterly otterly splashy surprise!

        We swim. We lope.
                We periscope.
        We loll. We romp. We fish
                and chomp.
        We roll. We pose.
                We put on shows.

We know you're pleased
to see us here.
You photograph us
everywhere!
In your rivers and on your shores—
We are the stars of Singapore!

As the island of Singapore was transformed into a modern city, roads and buildings rapidly replaced wetlands. The smooth-coated otter and other wildlife vanished. Understanding what they had lost, Singaporeans committed to a new vision of a "city in a garden" where plants, animals, and humans coexist. They planted one million trees. They removed a concrete channel and restored the natural riverbed and plants. Fish populations returned to healthy levels. Singapore is now over fifty percent green and hosts forty thousand species of animals and plants, including dragonflies, lizards, snakes, dolphins, cuckoos, herons, and eagles. When two smooth-coated otters appeared near downtown, they became a symbol of the city's green identity. The popular otters have adapted surprisingly well to urban life.

THE WORLD'S BIGGEST BEACH CLEANUP

Versova Beach, Mumbai, India

What *happened* to his beach?
  He remembers
childhood days,
   clean sand, blue waves.

Now he trudges through rubbish
 ankle-deep. It reeks.
It squishes beneath his feet.
 He plods past
  mounds of plastic
shoulder-high.
  Disgust.
  Despair.
At the water's edge,
 bags, bottles, rags
drift on the tide
where he used to swim and dive.
Sinking to his knees,
   Afroz Shah cries.

34

What can one man do?
He has to try!
He asks a friend.
That very day
their work begins
bend

scoop
stand
one handful at a time
the muck
the slime

What difference will it make?
How many decades will it take?
One weekend turns to three,
to five, to ten . . .
And then . . . at last . . .

May we join you? someone asks.
Then two, three, four
and more and more . . .

Now Afroz Shah has a crew
　that swarms the beach,
　fills buckets, bags,
trucks with trash.
Months go by.
　Another year.
　Another.
　　　Stop! Look around!

Clean sand
Pristine sand
As-far-as-the-eye-can-see-
　sand!

And then . . .
　eighty baby sea turtles
　wobble-crawl across the beach
　　and bobble-float into the sea.
　　A very, very sweet surprise!
　And sinking to his knees,
　　Afroz Shah cries.

Like many maritime species, olive ridley sea turtles are in decline due to climate change, fishing gear entanglement, hunters, pollution, and habitat destruction. They had disappeared from Versova Beach in Mumbai, India.

Afroz Shah led what the United Nations has called "the world's biggest beach cleanup." In 2018 an olive ridley sea turtle deposited her eggs on the newly cleaned up Versova Beach. Two months later, eighty hatchlings were spotted crawling across the sand, the first such sighting in thirty years.

HOW YOU CAN HELP

- **Start a nature journal**—observe the wildlife in your neighborhood.
- **Plant native plants**—create a pollinator garden in your yard, in window boxes, or in flowerpots.
- **Plant wildflower seeds**—make seed bombs and toss them into empty lots.
- **Provide water**—add birdbaths and water fountains to your patio, deck, or yard.
- **Provide healthy habitat**—stop using rakes and blowers. Leave leaf litter, rocks, branches, bushes, and even dead tree trunks in your garden for pollinators and small critters.
- **Protect wildlife from poisons**—avoid using pesticides, rodenticides, and other toxic products. Use natural alternatives.
- **Make your windows safe**—add decals and decorations to prevent bird collisions.
- **Keep the lights low**—use dimmer outdoor lighting that points downward. Find a Lights Out program in your city and learn how you can help.
- **Clean your city**—join a cleanup for a river, beach, park, or street, or start your own.
- **Start a school project**—talk to your classmates and teachers about creating a habitat garden in the schoolyard.
- **Support wildlife crossings**—write letters, make phone calls, or do a fundraiser to support wildlife crossing projects in your city.
- **Go natural**—find natural solutions instead of pesticides and rodenticides.
- **Plant trees**—join a tree-planting project or start your own. Ask city officials how you can help with planting and maintaining street trees.
- **Spread the word with creativity**—draw pictures, dance, or write poems, plays, or songs to celebrate urban wildlife.
- **Make it a neighborhood project**—get together with your neighbors to do all of the above.
- **Write and tell me what you're doing**—erica@ericasilverman.com.

MORE TO EXPLORE

Bronx River, New York: Beaver
- bronxriver.org/resource/an-evening-with-jose-the-bronx-river-beaver
- bronxriver.org/resource/beaver-castor-canadensis

Oslo, Norway, Pollinator Highway: Honeybees
- greenmatters.com/community/2017/08/29/Z1NfQBm/norway-creates-bee-highway-to-help-strengthen-biodiversity

Esperanza School, Los Angeles, California: Burrowing Owl
- socalwild.com/2016/12/burrowing-owl-delights-students-staff-at-urban-school/1816

London, UK, Green Roofs: Black Redstart
- dustygedge.co.uk/index.php/birds/black-redstarts-on-london-olympic-green-roof

Toronto, Canada: Ravens
- nationalpost.com/news/toronto/ravens-spotted-in-toronto-set-the-birding-world-abuzz

Australia: Western Possum
- abc.net.au/news/2019-06-29/first-possum-rope-bridge-in-perth-hailed-as-breakthrough/11258078
- abc.net.au/local/stories/2014/10/13/4105896.htm

Chicago, Illinois: Migrating Birds
Bird Collision Monitors:
- birdmonitors.net

Lights out Programs:
- audubon.org/conservation/existing-lights-out-programs

Window Protection:
- allaboutbirds.org/news/why-birds-hit-windows-and-how-you-can-help-prevent-it

El Segundo, California: Blue Butterfly
- esbcoalition.org

Oamaru, New Zealand: Penguins
- cnn.com/2016/11/12/asia/nz-penguin-underpass/index.html
- nathab.com/blog/videos-the-penguin-paths-of-new-zealand

Singapore: Otters
- facebook.com/ottercity
- youtube.com/watch?v=J7f6s2g8C0I
- crickeyamigudinatura.org/2022/12/13/cheeky-otters-are-thriving-in-singapore

Mumbai, India: Sea Turtles
- afrozshahfoundation.org

RESOURCES FOR FAMILIES AND EDUCATORS

Books

- Haupt, Lyanda Lynn. *The Urban Bestiary: Encountering the Everyday Wild.* New York: Little, Brown Spark, 2013.

- Marzluff, John M. and Jack DeLap. *Welcome to Subirdia: Sharing Our Neighborhoods with Wrens, Robins, Woodpeckers, and Other Wildlife.* New Haven: Yale University Press, 2015.

- Mizejewski, David. *National Wildlife Federation: Attracting Birds, Butterflies, and Other Backyard Wildlife*, expanded 2nd ed. Fox Chapel, PA: Design Originals, 2019.

- Tallamy, Douglas W. *Nature's Best Hope: A New Approach to Conservation That Starts in Your Yard.* Portland, OR: Timber Press, 2020.

- Wormser, Owen. *Lawns into Meadows: Growing a Regenerative Landscape.* San Francisco: Stone Pier Press, 2020.

Websites

- **Certify Your Habitat**
  Turn your yard into a wildlife habitat and get it certified!
  nwf.org/CertifiedWildlifeHabitat

- **Children and Nature**
  Support and resources for leaders, educators, activists, and parents working to turn the trend of an indoor childhood back out to the benefits of nature—and to increase safe and equitable access to the natural world for all.
  childrenandnature.org

- **Eco-Schools**
  A project of the National Wildlife Federation providing resources and curriculum to support students in building climate-resilient communities. They have inspired 9,900 yard habitats.
  nwf.org/eco-schools-usa

- **Eliminate Rodenticides**
  Raptors Are the Solution (RATS)
  raptorsarethesolution.org

- **Homegrown National Park**
  A movement to restore native ecosystems to yards and community spaces as an extension of the national parks. Participants can add their restored habitat to the interactive online map.
  homegrownnationalpark.org

- **iNaturalist**
  Everyone in the family can become a community scientist with this app. Take pictures of plants and animals and upload them to be counted as part of your city's ecosystem.
  inaturalist.org

- **Leave the Leaves**
  Learn how gardening without leaf blowers is better for pollinators and for everyone's health.
  xerces.org/blog/leave-the-leaves

- **Living Schoolyards Act**
  Learn what you can do to support this legislation that will help green our schoolyards.
  greenschoolyards.org/living-schoolyards-act

- **Native Plant Database, Audubon**
  audubon.org/native-plants

- **Native Plant Finder, National Wildlife Foundation**
  nwf.org/NativePlantFinder

- **Plant City Trees**
  onetreeplanted.org

- **Seed Bombs**
  How to make seed bombs.
  wildlifetrusts.org/actions/how-make-seed-bomb

- **Urban Wildlands Group**
  With links to multiple urban rewilding resources, the Urban Wildlands Group is dedicated to the protection of species, habitats, and ecological processes in urban and urbanizing areas.
  urbanwildlands.org/links.html

CHILDREN'S BOOKS CELEBRATING CITY WILDLIFE

- Brown, Peter. *The Curious Garden*. New York: Little, Brown Books for Young Readers, 2009.
- Bunting, Eve, and Ted Rand. *Secret Place*. New York: Clarion Books, 1996.
- Duffield, Katy S. *Crossings: Extraordinary Structures for Extraordinary Animals*. San Diego: Beach Lane Books, 2020.
- Guy, Cylita, and Cornelia Li. *Chasing Bats and Tracking Rats: Urban Ecology, Community Science, and How We Share Our Cities*. Toronto: Annick Press, 2021.
- Lappano, Jon-Erik, and Kellen Hatanaka. *Tokyo Digs a Garden*. Toronto: Groundwood Books, 2016.
- Larsen, Andrew, and Anne Villeneuve. *Me, Toma and the Concrete Garden*. Toronto: Kids Can Press, 2019.
- Lloyd, Megan Wagner, and Abigail Halpin. *Finding Wild*. New York: Knopf Books for Young Readers, 2016.
- Mulder, Michelle. *Going Wild: Helping Nature Thrive in Cities*. Victoria, BC: Orca Book Publishers, 2018.
- Pincus, Meeg, and Alexander Vidal. *Cougar Crossing: How Hollywood's Celebrity Cougar Helped Build a Bridge for City Wildlife*. San Diego: Beach Lane Books, 2021.
- Singer, Marilyn, and Gordy Wright. *Wild in the Streets: 20 Poems of City Animals*. London: words & pictures/Quarto, 2019.
- Thomson, Sarah L., and Douglas W. Tallamy. *Nature's Best Hope: How You Can Save the World in Your Own Yard*, young readers' ed. Portland, OR: Timber Press, 2023.
- Wahman, Wendy. *Old Pearl*. New York: Atheneum/Caitlyn Dlouhy Books, 2021.